Rank One

A.M.Spadaro

ISBN:1517618835
ISBN-13:9781517618834

DEDICATION

To my family: Jason, Pam, Emma, and Gianna, who believed
in my writing.

CONTENTS

ACKNOWLEDGMENTS

Great thanks to all my friends at school and at drama. You all are the true main characters.

KINGDOMS FALL

Just outside of the Milky Way lies a planet of fire., at least that's what we called it. Though it wasn't really on fire, we had three suns, so it made sense. Most of the planet was desert; though there were about 30 colonies. One representative of each would gather at the dome about once or twice a year to discuss business. The colony I grew up in, Bocs was very small and mainly farmed. My only family was my father, and he was on the council. I wasn't interested in learning things the other kids would fan over. Instead of farming, I learned fighting, with the intention of becoming the first female guard; instead of movies, I read books, trying to escape reality. I can't remember exactly, but I think it was around the 15th of May. When everything changed. My father had left for a council meeting while I was reading. Soon, people outside were running. I looked up and saw chaos. People were fleeing from the burning town.

I ran to the window and saw the library burn…There were robots, like tin men, heading towards the houses. I saw a few enter a house which I knew to belong to Samantha. Soon I heard a blast. I flinched, and the robot came out, blood smeared across its hands. My eyes widened and I ran out to Samantha's house. "SAM?!" I ran to where she lay, covered in blood.

"H-hey . . . Sav…" She coughed in pain.

"Shh…rest, my friend..." I couldn't help but cry.

Samantha struggled to say more, but couldn't. There was nothing I could do; her eyes soon closed. She was the closest I had to a friend. Out of anger I ran out of the house and started running to the council building. I was about half way there when someone grabbed me from behind. I turned around and saw a man with a bandana over his mouth and swords on his back. He had a tight grip on my arm, and stared at the building until more robots started to gather. The man went to fight them, providing me freedom, and I took this chance to run to the council building. I didn't get much closer when there was an explosion; fire shot bright out of the side and glass flew everywhere. "N-no…NO!!" I cried out.

"We have to go, Savanna!" I hadn't noticed at the time, but the stranger somehow knew my name.

I was too busy staring at the fire. Tears stained my face. "F-Father…"

I was twelve.

1.
A WEIRD BEGINNING

Roxy woke up with a start. She had had that dream of a girl losing her dad for a while now and each time it got sadder. Zurvocks was a quiet colony at the edge of all the others. It was known to have the best warriors, but Roxy wasn't a fighter. After all, she was the princess of Zurvocks. Her father, King Rory, was one of the most respected royals on the planet. Lately though, her father had said something had happened five years ago and things have changed. When Roxy had asked he simply said: "We're hiding."

Roxy hated when her father didn't tell her things. There was a knock on the door. "MA'AM? ARE YOU AWAKE?" Gong, the army General, yelled from the other side of the door.

"YES!" Roxy called back at his level of yelling.

"YOUR PACKAGE HAS ARRIVED, MISS" He continued to yell.

"Oh goody! My dresses!" She paused, "And Gong, you don't have to yell."

"UNDER-...Ahem, understood." With that he left back for his post as two servants brought a box to her room and started putting the dresses away.

When they finished they and left, Roxy went to her closet. *What to wear…what to wear…* She chose an aqua dress to compliment her blonde hair and blue eyes. She put it on and twirled. Roxy sat by her window and thought about the dream. She had had crazier ones, but they never repeated. Staring outside she watched Zach run. He had ginger hair and hazel eyes. He was soon followed by a larger group that kept growing. "What the…" She whispered in confusion.

Roxy stared before robots came into view and they were attacking HER loyal subjects. They shot lasers and spread fire. One robot looked up and caught her gaze. She heard the robot command: "Get the girl, Framil Framil."

She turned around, her hair flying in her face and headed towards the door. She was too late, more of these 'Framils' were already entering her room. She backed up until she fell onto her bed. She closed her eyes, expecting the worst. Instead, Roxy heard a sawing noise and she looked up. Someone was carving a hole in her roof with a sword. The ceiling part fell down and broke and a girl jumped down. "Hope I'm not late to the party!"

"You are actually pretty early. Framil. Framil." One of the robots squeaked.

The girl nodded. She had shoulder-length black hair with brown at the ends. She was wearing a black tank top that said F.R.E.E. and jeans. The girl had a bandana over her mouth, but Roxy could see that her eyes were green. This girl had what looked like one third of a perfectly straight stick in her hand. She pressed a button on this 'stick' and two blades came out. She jumped forward and drove one of the blades into the first robot. Turning around, she easily sliced the second robot. Roxy stared in confusion as this strange girl sliced up the oncoming robots or 'Framils'. *Is she one of my guards?* She thought. *No…Girls can't be guards…* the girl finished slicing and walked to Roxy, taking off the bandana. "You need to come with me, now."

"Why? You're not the boss of me! You're just a lowly peasant!" Roxy threw a pillow at her.

Without looking the girl threw a shuriken at an oncoming Framil. "That's why."

Roxy's face didn't change. *Ugh…I don't get paid to deal with this!* The girl thought. She whistled to a helicopter and a ladder came down. "Listen, Miss Prissy, Zurvocks is one of the twenty kingdoms that hasn't fallen, yet. Now it's in the process of falling. The whole kingdom has been evacuated except you. Now, get up the ladder before I leave you here for Jensen to kill you or turn you into one of those." She pointed at the robots.

"Humph! How dare you threaten the Princess of Zurvocks! I'm only going to see my Dad and then he can decide what to do with you." Roxy climbed up the ladder and the girl rolled her eyes and soon followed.

Roxy sat uncomfortable on a seat of the helicopter while the girl held onto the roof and stood on the edge. "What's your name?" Roxy asked.

"Savanna."

"You don't talk much do you?"

"Actions speak louder than words." Savanna strapped herself into a parachute and jumped out leaving a note that said 'follow me'.

Panicked, Roxy got help from a soldier and prepared to jump. Roxy stood on the edge too much and she fell without warning. Savanna glided down to a tree that parted and revealed a landing pad with a trampoline. Meanwhile, Roxy finally found the lever and pulled it, releasing the parachute. She barely landed on the trampoline. Savanna had already gotten the parachute off and was waiting for Roxy. Roxy struggled to get out of the parachute and angrily punched Savanna on the left side of her head. Savanna didn't flinch. "WHAT WAS THAT FOR?!" Roxy yelled.

"Did 'ye royal highness' never learn to jump off of a helicopter?" Savanna looked confused as if everyone should know that.

"No, we don't! I don't know where you came from, but here in Zurvocks, we aren't all soldiers!" Roxy fumed.

Savanna didn't reply, but instead started walking towards a hidden staircase. She typed in a code and the door opened. She walked down the stairs with a still angry Roxy following. "Fourth level is yoga. Third is shooting range. Second is housing. First is control room and basement is the training arena."

Savanna kept walking until they arrived at the control room, many people wearing the same black F.R.E.E. shirts.

"Hey, what does F.R.E.E. stand for?" Roxy asked as she noticed it was written everywhere.

"Fighters Reaching for Everlasting Enlightenment. We fight for peace and nothing else. War should not be desired." Savanna looked on gravely.

The control room had camera monitors and fire alarms, normal things. Roxy looked at one camera which showed two guys sparring. This first guy was smaller and appeared to be losing before he kicked the other guy into a support beam and punched him square in the nose. Roxy flinched and Savanna was off signing papers about who Roxy was. "DRI!!" Savanna called.

A girl with brown, boy-short hair ran up to Savanna. She was also wearing a F.R.E.E. shirt and jeans. She had a clipboard and brown eyes. "Yes?"

"Show Miss Prissy to her room, please." Savanna asked, "I have to check on the mission status."

"MY NAME IS ROXY!!" Roxy was furious for being treated this way.

"Come along, Miss. You've been through a lot." Dri lead Roxy away to her room on the top floor.

"Now THAT'S how I should be treated! With respect!" Roxy blurted without noticing that Dri flinched and broke her pencil.

"Right through here…Miss Pr-…never mind…" Dri mumbled through gritted teeth.

Roxy sauntered into the room and slammed the door in Dri's face. Walking over to the far left, she sat on the bed that had plain beige color. Across from this bed there was a plain grey wall with a lever. Curious, Roxy got up and pulled the lever which caused a part of the wall to fall and reveal a wide array of weapons. Roxy ran her hand down the side of a sword blade before wandering some more. She walked over to a curtain and moved it aside. Beyond the curtain was a closet full of dresses and skirts, a few pairs of leggings, too. There was a note on the wall next to the closet that read:

Some clothes we found that might suit you

If you don't like it, don't wear it

No refunds on saving your life.

Meet me in the training arena

At 2.

-S

Roxy crumpled up the piece of paper and threw it away, mentally burning it. She looked at the time and thought. *Hope she doesn't kill me for being late…*

2.
RUN FOR YOUR LIFE

It was 2:30 by the time Roxy had found the note. It took even more time to change and leave her room. She didn't want to ask any of these 'lowly peasants that shouldn't get paid' where to go. She wanted to show them that she belonged anywhere. She kept a sharp eye out for her father, though. She made her way to the elevator. Stepping in, she pressed the button that said 'Training arena' and waited. It didn't work. The doors were about to go when a boy with red hair and green eyes ran into the elevator. "Zach?! They dragged you into this too?" Roxy Screeched.

"No, I've always worked for F.R.E.E. Why? Is that a bad thing?" Zack stared confused.

Ugh...Only for Zach... Roxy thought before forcing a smile and leaning against the elevator wall. "N-no! I ...I.I...love it here!" She cringed.

He stared skeptically before shaking his head. "Where to?"

"This elevator works?!" Roxy half screamed, standing straight up again.

"Yeah, but you can't operate it. The buttons respond to finger prints. Yours aren't in the system, yet." Zach pressed basement. *He must be going there too.*

She nodded, trying to understand this strange organization. After some awkward stares and silence, the elevator finally made it to the basement and they got out. She got a good look at the training arena. On her left there was a room with a glass window in front to observe people. In front of the elevator were two ways down: a steel crossway that lead to a staircase or a rock wall to climb down. The steel was rusted at some parts, but it looked sturdy enough. Roxy walked across the creaking bridge to the stairs and ran down hurriedly. She looked at the arena itself. The walls were rocks and dirt fused with steel and metal. There were bioluminescent lights hanging from the ceiling. There were separate fighting mats; some had blood on them from really bad fights. Various weapons were spread out between different racks. There were assorted training obstacles too. Monkey bars, tires to jump in, rope swings, barbed wire to crawl under. *Am I sure this isn't a military base?* Roxy wondered. She walked to the back, out of place amongst the fighters. She soon found Savanna and watched her for a bit before interrupting. Savanna was fighting an older male that was about ten times her size. She ducked under his arm as he swung at her with his fist. She kicked him in the back and he fell, but soon got up again. He had blood on his lips and when Savanna kicked at him he caught her foot. She slammed her foot down dragging him with her. With her other foot she slammed it down on his head causing him to black out. "Whoa…" Roxy admired the escape.

"Huh? Oh, you're finally here!" Savanna dried her hands with a towel.

"What? Oh yeah, you need to change the elevator process!" Roxy let out a sigh; *Thank goodness she's not mad…*

"It's a safety procedure, I'll need to give you access after we're done here." Savanna pointed to the track that ran around the entire room. "Five laps, go."

"What?! You're making ME run?!" Roxy said in shock.

"Yes." Savanna was unfazed by Roxy's obvious anger at the exercise.

Roxy stormed off to the track in rage, Savanna didn't even blink. Roxy didn't start running until she realized the track had traps. She first found this when she was strolling along the first wall. She was about a quarter of the way when the floor split open and she was forced back to the start, unless she wanted to fall into the lava below. A rope swung about twenty feet above the lava. The way it was set, it looked like there was no way she could reach it. "HOW THE HECK AM I SUPPOSED TO REACH THAT!?!" Roxy yelled over the commotion.

"SIMPLE. IF YOU RAN, YOU COULD'VE HAD THE FORCE TO JUMP AND GRAB THE ROPE WITH ENOUGH MOMENTUM TO SWING OVER." Savanna had cleared this course many times.

Roxy jogged back to the beginning of the course. Other runners had smirks on their faces as they ran and easily jumped to the rope and over to the other side. *I'll show them*, +Roxy thought as she got on the mark. She waited until she had Savanna's full attention. When Savanna looked, Roxy took off sprinting. She felt the wind and the stares. She was already losing her breath, she had never run this fast. She soon reached the pit where the lava burned a bright orange. She bent her knees and jumped as high as she could. The height was not the problem- Roxy ended up to far too the left and she missed the rope. The platform quickly closed and she landed flat on her back and rear end. Pain surged through her lower half as she stood up and saw the other runners staring at her. She got up and ran towards what she believed to be the bathrooms. Ignoring the pain in her back she opened the door and stepped in. "Thank goodness this IS the bathroom…"

There was a knock on the door and Savanna walked in without Roxy's say. Roxy was leaning on the counter, facing the sink. She refused to look at the mirror in case she saw Savanna's face or worse, her own. Savanna, without a word, lifted the back of Roxy's shirt and checked her back for blood. "If you bleed we need to know, in case…*something*…gets its nasty hands on your DNA."

"Well I'm not bleeding; I think I'd feel it!" Roxy snapped.

"Emotions can block pain more than you think, *Princess*." The word sounded tart coming from Savanna's mouth.

After checking for any cuts, Savanna left as quietly as she came. Roxy thought for a moment then looked up at the mirror. Her blue eyes screamed of hate and embarrassment. They were on the verge of tears as well. Her blonde hair was matted and dirty, but her clothes were much worse. Sleeves torn away and she had lost her shoes. After she had changed into a red tank top and jean shorts she started to realize that the only clothes here were commoner clothes. "Not much variety in dresses…Like they couldn't be even more poor."

Roxy washed her face and walked out with her chin in the air and a proud strut. She wasn't about to let them think their running antics would get the best of her. When she neared the running track, she took off in a sprint and headed for the pit. She jumped and this time grabbed the rope. Her hands slipped a bit and she barely made it over. When her feet hit the mat on the other side she took off running and stumbling. She slowed to a stop and looked back at the pit she had crossed. A smile crept onto her face. Savanna walked over and stood in front of Roxy. "Was that so hard?"

Roxy squinted, "Um, YES! What the heck, Sav?!"

Savanna flinched. "Don't. Call. Me. That."

"Oh is there something that can actually bother this 'oh-so-perfect' leader of F.R.E.E.?" Drawing air quotes with her fingers.

Savanna shot forward and pinned Roxy against the wall with her arm over Roxy's throat. "Listen here, brat!" Savanna's voice became quiet and harsh, "If you want to stay alive and human, you better listen to the rules and to me because I am the only thing keeping you alive on this forsaken planet that is sentenced to doom. You think you know what's going on? You are so wrong. This world is spinning too fast for the news to travel I guess!"

Roxy was about to speak when a small device at Savanna's waist buzzed and blinked red. Savanna closed her eyes- her very piercing green eyes- and released Roxy. Roxy stood there dumbfounded while Savanna looked at the beeping, silver device. Savanna's eyes shot wide open when she looked at the message. "Twice in the same week?! The same DAY even!?"

"What? What is it?" Roxy tried to look at the message, but Savanna recoiled.

"Go to your room and don't follow anyone you don't know. DRI! PACK A BAG!" Savanna yelled and ran up to the balcony.

Dri ran over and nodded. "Who's the poor soul now?"

Savanna whispered, so only Dri could hear, "Lost Prince Mace. He doesn't know he's a Prince though, so don't tell him."

"Understood." Dri said. This was all Roxy heard before they dashed off to the stairs, both covering their faces with the same bandana Savanna had worn when she rescued Roxy.

3.
THE RESCUE

Dri was used to sudden missions. That's mostly all of what they did. Savanna had always talked about the revolution that would soon come, but then she would quickly follow up with, "But we're not ready yet."

Dri had asked multiple times throughout a year's span when they would be ready and Savanna only replied with, "Soon".

Now missions weren't a problem, but when Penich starts attacking two quadrants in one day? Armageddon. Dri had never heard of this Prince Mace, which was very strange, but she was sure anything was better than that stuck up girly girl. Besides, he didn't even know he's a prince, so he couldn't have been that bad, right? Dri kept pace with Savanna as they ran up the stairs to the helipad. The helicopter was ready to go when they got there which meant Savanna had informed the pilots. They didn't need to talk to each other to know that Dri usually scouted and kept others off Savanna's trail while Savanna attacked and received the royalty. They hopped on the helicopter and it took off into the sky. Half an hour passed before they arrived to a burning town. Flames licked the sky as smoke blocked the helicopter's path. "WE'RE GOING TO HAVE TO FIGHT OUR WAY THROUGH!!" Savanna yelled over the noise.

Dri nodded and hooked a rope to the landing bar. She slid down the rope and landed on a roof. She sprinted across the rooftops until she got a good vantage point and she spotted the main building. She reported to Savanna through an intercom. "Center of a crossway, big cylinder…uh…thing? Dang it! THE GAINT FLAMING WATER CUP IN THE MIDDLE!"

Savanna laughed and swung on the rope over to the building. Dri kept a sharp lookout before shortly following and blocking the entrance door, so Savanna wouldn't be followed. Inside, Savanna ducked behind some crates labeled with metals and fire arms. She peeked around the left side of one of the crates and saw what she was tracking. The Prince Mace was trapped in a glass cylinder as a sort of cyborg Framil creature paced in front of a control panel. Mace had short brown hair that was cut close to his head. He wore a black T-shirt with a game controller on it and jeans. His shoes had been taken from him, but he didn't seem to notice. The only thing his brown eyes showed was fear. The cyborg was what looked like a former army general. His grey eyes were stern and his buzz cut was short and tight. Most of his body was metal, with the exception of the left half of his face and right arm. He was one of the only Framils or Framil like creatures that didn't have designed metal. The designs on the metal showed the Framil's rank. Swirls around the arm usually meant small missions and guard duties. Zigzagged and computer patterns meant great missions and killing duties. No pattern meant they were one of the Penich's main Framil's and they were very important. Savanna's head swirled with plans, most involving a distraction of some sort. She was about to initiate plan number 223 when Roxy crashed through the ceiling. "What the-?" Savanna started before the cyborg turned and scanned Roxy.

"HEY! IDIOT! OVER HERE!" Roxy lit a flare and

waved it around.

Savanna face-palmed silently, "He's a cyborg; not a dog…"

"Roxy Metorme. Age 15. Height 5'3". Origin in Zurvocks; Rank: Princess. Command: Capture and reform." The cyborg's voice was deep and raspy.

"Uh…What?" Roxy's stance dropped and she looked confusedly at the Framil.

Savanna took the time to sneak around behind the cyborg. She was about halfway to the cylinder before the robot turned around and scanned her. "Savanna Eteron. Age 17. Height 5'10". Origin in Bocs; Rank: Officer's daughter. Command: Kill."

Outside, Dri had heard the crash and was now standing in the doorway, a bow and arrow at the ready. "Not on my watch." She stated and the robot turned to her.

"Z-" The robot started before Dri fired the arrow and it hit the cyborg in its human eye. The cyborg started to buzz. "Bzzt…zzziitt…BZZZ!!!"

Dri turned her head away as blood and oil spilled from the Framil's eye, "Get Mace."

Savanna nodded and walked the rest of the way to Mace, while Roxy stared at the cyborg in horror. Dri ran to Roxy, "His name is Quinn. If you want to sit there and pity the guy that was going to kill Savanna. Now, you stowed away if I am correct. So, if you want to stay alive then you should get back to the helicopter before Savanna personally kills you."

Mace had now stood up and Savanna got a better view of his legs. He wasn't missing his shoes, he just couldn't wear them. Savanna pondered of when Quinn had turned Mace's "Well that was unexpected..." Savanna said.

"What? Was I supposed to yell out something like "Oh? Hey! Yeah I've got robot legs now! Ain't that cool?" He added with a cheesy smile.

"No. I just don't know when Quinn did that before Dri attacked. I didn't see it."

"Nah that's okay. He started the process, but the machine went on the frits and he had to stop it. That's why he was pacing."

Just then a blaring alarm went off and the building went into lockdown. Red lights flashed and the glass around Mace was closed off by a steel surrounding. Roxy and Dri rushed to the door. Roxy was screaming in fear, "WE'RE GONNA DIE! WE'RE GONNA DIE!"

Dri got annoyed after five minutes of this and slapped Roxy. "Get a hold of yourself solider! It's just an alarm! It's not certain doom yet!"

Savanna rolled her eyes and inspected the now, steel cylinder. *Well I can't leave him...* She thought before a banging sound from inside the cylinder started. Inside, Mace was screaming 'MOVE', but to no avail. He was kicking at the steel and it started to break. When it burst open, Savanna held up her arms to shield the flying debris, although she did get cut in several places; mostly her face. "I guess that works..." She mumbled.

Dri slow clapped behind her. Just when she was about to clap for the sixth time, Quinn had removed the arrow and tackled Dri. He pressed his metal arm to her throat and laughed as she prepared for death. *You've been over this, in case of death, remain calm and accept it. Years and years of training will catch up and you'll make it out…* She thought as she relayed a plan. Roxy side-tackled Quinn and Dri stared up in shock. Mace hobbled over to Roxy and Quinn and punched Quinn's back, "STOP TUMBLING!!" He yelled and then swiftly recoiled, "Ow! Ow! Owie! Robots hurt…"

Quinn threw Roxy aside and stood up. Savanna ran around to Quinn's back and jumped up, stabbing the arrow in between the flesh and wires. Quinn screamed and his flesh began to melt due to the electricity surging out of the broken wires. The skin melted off first, dripping down the metal, leaving blood stains and muscles that were torn in half. The skin bubbled and seared to the ground, leaving only bones and ripped muscles crushed beneath the metal. In the corner of the room, Roxy puked and Mace turned away. Savanna stood there, gasping. Dri, however, walked to the mess of meat and metal and poked it. "Can I take it in for sampling?" She asked with a smile.

Savanna nodded, covering her mouth, "We need to go. I think I'm going to be sick…" She took a moment to compose herself. "To the helicopter, poor Manny's been waiting this whole time."

They headed back to the helicopter with Mace, still a bit nervous about the whole 'world is ending' thing. While they were flying, Savanna walked to Dri, who was standing in a corner. She didn't face her, but Savanna whispered to Dri: "Why did Quinn start calling you Z?"

"I don't know," She replied, "Must've been a glitch or something."

Savanna nodded. "Huh…Okay, well just wondering."

4.
TRAINING

No one looked back until the building they were just in exploded. Roxy and Mace jumped while Savanna glanced back; Dri had fallen asleep. "So, where are we going?" Mace asked.

"The only place that's safe, even though it's not safe enough." Savanna replied.

"What do you mean 'not safe enough'?!" Roxy jumped up from the box she was sitting on. "Do you mean to say that us, who are so very 'precious'", She air quoted here. "Are staying in a place that could get us killed?!"

Savanna looked up like she was thinking, then quickly replied with, "Yep! That's exactly what's going on!" with a smile.

Mace's jaw dropped and Roxy fumed some more. "What!? That's not exactly how this whole 'revolution' thing works! You save the person who saves the planet, a.k.a. me, and you keep them somewhere safe while they grow strong enough to take down the enemy!"

"What book have you been reading? Fairytales for the Blind Mind?" Savanna raised an eyebrow at Roxy. "Look, honey, this is not a fairytale or reading book. You're not the hero. You're bait unless you prove useful. No one is a hero and no one is rebelling. All we do is stave the important people, then we are leaving to find a new planet. The oldest one in this

21

ragtag group is twenty and blind. We can't stand up to them! They have an army; we have a fire and rescue squad."

Roxy sat back down on the box, her eyes downcast. The helicopter landed this time, giving that Dri was sleeping and Mace was still trying to get used to his new legs. Savanna shook Dri awake and Dri immediately jumped up and assumed fighting position. "There's no fire." Roxy blurted.

"Thanks, Captain Obvious." Dri countered, glaring at Roxy.

Roxy glared back. "Whoa! Glare fest…I'll just…go" Mace said, hopping out of the helicopter, with Savanna following behind, ready to give him a tour.

Dri and Roxy stared at each other before Roxy gave in and stood up to leave. "Watch your tongue little sprite." She said while jumping out of the helicopter and walking to the elevator.

*   *   *

After all of the day's work, everyone went to bed. At the crack of dawn, Savanna woke up and rolled off her be,. "If you can't get out of bed, you can't get out of trouble…"

She rolled onto her back and looked up at the ceiling of her room. Her room was standard, like everyone else's except she lived at the base so hers had clothing that she had picked out herself. She thought for a moment about how she was going to train Mace and Roxy. *Maybe Dri can train one and I can train the other? No…Dri doesn't seem to like them much and I can't train them in all the weapons. Maybe Dri can teach them archery and some attack plans. While I can train them in swordsmanship and hand-to-hand combat.* "That should work…"

"What should work?" Dri asked, standing at the door with a clipboard.

"Training procedures. Are you okay with teaching them attack plans and ranged fighting?" Savanna tilted her head to look at Dri.

"As long as I'm not training both at the same time."

"Nah, I've got a plan for that. Roxy with you for the first two parts of fighting while Mace is with me, then we switch trainees." Savanna stated while getting up off the floor.

"I shall bring them to the training arena." Dri nodded and headed off to their rooms.

All the rooms were on the same floor, although there were boy and girl sections. She headed to the boy's side first since she hated Mace less and knocked on his door. Mace opened the door, still dressed in the same clothes as yesterday, and stepped out. "I'm guessing I'm wanted because no one has knocked. They usually barge in for everything that's not important."

"Strange," Dri motioned for him to follow as she walked. "I'll ask them about that. They should be knocking, but I guess only certain people keep to proper manners when under the destruction of a planet."

Mace looked at Dri in confusion; he was taller than the 5'7" girl, but not by much. He shook his head and waited by the Neither/Both section until Dri walked back from the girl's section with a very grouchy Roxy following her. Mace trailed behind for a bit before poking Roxy. "Someone wake up on the wrong sun?" He smirked.

"Yes, and if you poke me one more time you won't be able to poke anymore!"

In front of them Dri started laughing. "Ah…petty fights like this make me understand how naive the people on this planet are!"

She entered the elevator and waited for the others to follow. They stood there for a minute before entering. At the last moment, Zach sauntered into the elevator. "Solider." Dri winked at him.

*How dare she flirt with him! Wait…Why am I jealous?! He's just a commoner…a cute commoner…*Roxy shook her head trying to clear her absurd thoughts. Mace acted like nothing was wrong, which made Roxy mad. The elevator ride seemed to be longer than when Roxy first went to the training arena. Maybe it was the awkward silence. Roxy sighed relief only when the doors opened and they walked out. Savanna was waiting on the bridge, writing in a journal. Dri walked up to Savanna first and nudged her. Savanna's head shot up and she slammed the journal shut. "Oh! You're here."

"Yes and I've brought Zack with me." Dri motioned for Zack to step forward.

"Why?" Savanna looked him up and down.

"I can't make it to training...err...teaching. An urgent matter came up recently that I have to personally attend to because you are not able to." Dri then walked away without getting Savanna's approval.

"Wait...So, you knew about training us and THAT'S why she winked at you?" Roxy said, thinking aloud.

"Yes. Is there a problem with winking?" Zack stared down at Roxy.

Over by where he was standing by himself, Mace started laughing into his hand. "I-I'm sorry..." He said in between laughs, "Wow, you are dense, buddy! Spitfire over here thinks Dri was flirting with you!"

Zach's face flushed as he stammered, "WH-what? No no no no no no! Sorry man, you know how I don't understand girls!"

"I know." Mace was still laughing.

Savanna was laughing, but Roxy stood there very confused; she shook her head again and regained her posture. Savanna explained how she would train them in swordsmanship and hand-to-hand combat and Zach would teach attack plans and archery. They parted ways and began their training.

Savanna took Mace first and Zach took Roxy. Savanna had Mace practice with real swords. "What if I get hurt?"

"Walk it off." She shrugged.

"What if I die?"

"Walk it off."

Mace sighed and followed her instructions about how 'proper fighting' worked. It was about as proper as trying to teach a giraffe how to stand on two legs. At his first test of fighting, Mace made the mistake of jumping to avoid a punch. This gave Savanna the chance to pull his leg, literally, causing him to fall flat on his back. Savanna started laughing, "Never do anything that the opponent can take advantage of."

"Well, I'm sorry that I'm not a superstar in war." Mace stuttered.

"No duh!" Savanna laughed before holding out her hand to help him stand.

Mace stared at her hand then back to her. He slowly reached his hand out and accepted her help up. "PHSYCHE!" Savanna yelled as she pulled Mace up and flung him over her shoulder.

"ACK!" Mace screamed as his back slammed onto the concrete. "What was that for!?"

"I literally JUST said don't do anything that the opponent can take advantage of!" Savanna said between laughs.

"I didn't know we were still fighting after you knocked me down…" Mace cringed, standing up.

"Awe, my bad. Do you want me to tell the bad guys to take it easy on you?" Savanna talked in a baby voice.

Alright bad girl…let's go. Mace thought before fake walking away. He got to a point at which Savanna thought he was leaving and then he quickly turned around and smacked the back of her head with his palm. Savanna started to fake cry to try and mess with him. "Ha-ha. I'm not falling for your trick. You're stronger than that." Mace said while he put Savanna in a head lock and waited for her to say something.

"Alright you got me. I think that's a good enough lesson for now. LET'S TAKE IT FROM THE TOP!"

*   *   *

Throughout the entire training session with Roxy and Zach, Roxy could not keep her eyes off of Zach. He, of course was always focused on the weapons. He didn't seem to notice any of her subtle flirting. She thought that when all of this was over, he could possibly be her king, but the oblivious will do as the oblivious must. He started talking about the bow and the angle it should be at in order to get a good shot sixty percent of the time, meanwhile, Roxy watching him with disapproval and anger due to his stupidity. *Doesn't matter, right?* Roxy thought. *If he looks good, he is good.*

"And that's how you fire an arrow!" Zach finished.

Roxy shot to attention and pretended she caught all the information he gave her. "Alright! Say, are you free tonight?"

Zach thought for a second. "Well, I'm not in jail, so I would say yes." He chuckled.

Roxy, who did not think this was funny, stormed off angrily just in time for Dri to get back from her mission. "Wait! What did I say?" Zach asked, confused.

Dri laughed, "Oh, you lovable idiot." She said then walked off to find Savanna leaving Zack standing alone.

Dri found Savanna just as Mace finished his training. Mace and Dri waved to each other, but continued walking their own ways. Savanna had started hitting a punching bag. Dri waited until Savanna stopped before walking any further. "Where did you go for this 'mission'?" Savanna asked.

"Just a little beyond our protective barriers." Dri replied.

"For you, a little could mean a mile. Was it recon?"

"Yes."

"What did you find?"

"They are holding people captive. Not everyone in the prison block has been identified yet," Dri got quieter making sure only Savanna heard. "But, they have Zack's boyfriend in there."

5.
TROUBLE

Savanna froze and thought it over. "We can't let Zack know..."

"Why not?"

"We're almost ready to leave and he's at the main prison block. If we tried to save him more lives will be lost than the lives gained."

"Well what if we fight back?" Dri looked stern. "We could rebel. I mean you already train everyone like soldiers so why not let them be the warriors you've trained them to be? I can see it in your eyes, you are a general. You are meant to lead an army. You can lead that army. What's stopping you?"

"Everything." Savanna stood up and left, not bothering to wait for Dri.

Dri watched her boss walk away. She stretched and started training. She didn't care if Savanna wasn't going to do anything, she was.

*   *   *

Mace had been taking apart and putting his legs back together, trying to figure out how to build more legs. He was just about to give up looking for weaknesses when Dri walked in. "Mace."

"Yes ma'am?"

"Your legs are made from the same materials the Framils are. I want you to ignore any of Savanna's previous orders and find out what hurts them. We need to find a weakness for the Framils. To defeat them."

Mace nodded and Dri left to find Zack. She found him making hot chocolate, seemingly in deep thought"Zack."

"Yeah?" He looked up from his cup and looked at her.

"You're good with weapons. I want you to find Mace and help him study his machinery to see what can harm these stupid sentries. Once you do that, start creating new weapons to take out the Framils. Don't let Savanna know."

Zack didn't understand the secrecy, but he nodded anyways and took off to find Mace. Roxy who was nearby and heard the conversation soon walked up behind Dri and tapped her shoulder. "Anything you want me to do secretly?"

"No. You have not proven yourself useful."

"What are you talking about? I showed you all I could jump and run your stupid obstacle course!"

"Maybe so, but you still didn't pay attention during your training. You were too busy flirting with an unavailable guy." Dri sassed and walked away.

"I hate this place!" Roxy fumed.

＊   ＊   ＊

Mace had found a type of metal that could penetrate the surface of his leg, although it did not damage the inside. "Is there anything we can do to actually damage them?"

"Well the metal that penetrated your leg is not easily broken down. Which means acid can't hurt it. Although acid would do a number on your systems." Dri said

"So, we put the acid in the arrow?" Mace asked, lost.

"Exactly. Then fire the arrow into a Framil and probably create some sort a mechanism that could release the acid into the Framil. Maybe something attached to the bow?" Zach walked back around with a bow, examining the positions.

Mace hopped over and examined the bow as well, "Maybe we should put it near the firing part...so they could shoot n' shock!"

"Catchy. Though I don't think electricity would be effective."

Dri walked in, "What do you have for me?"

Zach stood at attention which caused Mace, who was leaning against him, to fall down. "WOAH!!"

"We figured that if we could fill the arrows with acid and make the arrows out of rhodium then we could press a button similar to how Earth car keys work with cars. The button would open the tip of the arrow-you know the pointy part here- and the acid would spill out." Zack explained while bouncing up and down like a kid.

Dri smiled and shook her head. "Well gather some people and start production, you can lead the group."

Zach saluted and ran off. Mace had now gotten off the floor and he looked around before seeing Savanna behind Dri. "Five o' clock, Dri." He whispered before walking away to join Mace.

"Hello Savanna." Dri spun on her heal and bowed.

Dri turned, but didn't get too far before Savanna grabbed her arm. "What are you doing?"

"I am going to…clear out my room." Dri was caught off guard by the question, but remained calm.

"Didn't you already pack up your entire armory?" Savanna raised an eyebrow and crossed her arms. "You're also facing the wrong way."

"That's because I was going to make sure everyone else cleared out first, these people are slow." Dri also crossed her arms and slowed her breath.

"Whatever." Savanna glared and walked back to her evacuation.

*   *   *

Roxy was at her room thinking about this place. *They lack enthusiasm…* "And yet they are still better than you." *That's funny considering you've known me longer.* "At least they do their job." *What are you talking about? I have been giving great advice.* "Yeah right since when did 'You should kill this person' or 'this one is so dead when I get them!' count as good advice?" *At least I'm not flirting with someone who was already stated as taken.* "He won't be taken for long if his boyfriend stays in jail."

*   *   *

Zach stared at his new contraption in wonder and appreciation. "Can you believe what simple, preschool technology can make?!" He mused to Mace, who was helping next to him.

"I'm not exactly Connor. I don't understand your guys' obsession per-say." Mace struggled to finish another arrow as he leaned on his lopsided leg.

Zach lowered his head at the mention of his boyfriend. He set the arrow on the table which caused Mace to look up. "Hey I'm sorry…I forgot…I didn't mean to bring him up…"

"No it's ok. I've accepted it by now." Zack leaned against the table and stared out at the other workers. "Where do you think he is?"

Mace patted him on the back, "Probably somewhere better."

*   *   *

Connor sat in the rusting cell. He was bruised and broken, but he didn't care. He took out the picture of his boyfriend that he had snuck in underneath his F.R.E.E. armband. That's why he's still alive. They are using him as bait, ever since he proved himself not breaking even when being tortured. "Please don't fall for it…"

*   *   *

Roxy walked over to Dri, speaking carefully, "How safe is this place?"

Dri continued working on some papers, file work that she wished she didn't have to do. "As safe as it can be, though it's not safe enough."

"Yeah are you ever going to fix that?" She asked. "I mean I don't care about you guys, but my life actually matters?"

Dri frowned at her clipboard. "Excuse me?"

Roxy nodded. "You heard me. I'm important. You know because I'm the only Princess, so my safety should be a priority."

Dri stared at her before laughing, slowly at first before bursting into a mocking laugh. "You're gaining a sense of humor! That's wonderful. We need more of that these days."

"What?! I'm being serious here! I am a Princess and should be respected of the highest order! You are all nothing to me! Just peasants!"

Dri stood up; she was taller than Roxy, so she could easily glare down at the smaller girl. "Sorry to break it to you honey but, THIS IS WAR!! There is no Peasants or Princesses! No royalty or slaves! When it's such a fine line between life and death, people don't get roles! They get a job on the field where people fight for their freedom and most of the time, lose their lives. This is not a game, at all."

Roxy flinched and stepped back once, though she kept a straight face, trying not to lose her composure. "Listen, this war is going to continue and when it's over, I'm going to be there and as the only royalty left, I presume I will be in charge. I know that running a planet can be a burden, but I'm sure Zack will make a good King by my side."

"Are you freaking kidding me?!" Dri laughed again, covering her eyes. "HOW BLIND ARE YOU?!?"

"Excuse me?" Roxy frowned and her eyebrows furrowed together.

"HE'S GAY!!" Dri smiled as if it was the most obvious thing in the world.

"H-he's...what..?" Roxy's eyes widened. "No...he's not, he just...he just hasn't found the right girl yet!"

"Ok, that's wrong he's literally dating a guy, like I've seen them kiss." Dri raised an eyebrow and held up her hand before Roxy could speak again. "And don't even start to say things like 'Oh he loves me anyway' or 'Maybe he's Bisexual and hasn't noticed it before!' Because honey, he's one of the gayest people I know and I know a lot of people."

Savanna laughed behind Roxy and walked over. "Great story, but we need to evacuate and I just checked your place, Roxy. It's not cleared out."

"You expect *me* to clean out that mucky stall?"

"Yes, that's exactly as you were supposed to do and before you go into another 'high and mighty' speech, you don't mean as much as you think you do here. Here you are equal at most." Savanna turned to Dri, "As for you, I will need you to help me get some of these weapons out of the basement, we need to be prepared."

Dri nodded as Savanna left, hoping Mace and Zack could keep her distracted from the new weapons they were creating. Roxy was aghast from being talked to like that and she pushed back her bangs. "If that's what I am *at most*, then what am I at least?"

While she was leaving to stop Savanna, Dri half shouted to Roxy, "A burden."

Savanna was at the elevators before Dri had caught up. Dri, at first remained quiet until the elevator arrived, then she spoke up, "Hey, maybe we should assign the weapons job to someone else…I mean you are the leader and you should be up top, leading us! This is how it's supposed to go, isn't it?"

Savanna considered it, "Fine. At least let me get something I forgot in my office. While I do that, you can organize people to get the weapons."

Dri nodded nervously and texted Mace and Zack on her phone. The message read: GUYS! Sav is going to her office. Stop process and make it look like you're packing weapons to ship them out. Savanna looked over at her phone, trying to read it and Dri put it back in her pocket. "Just telling them to pack up."

"You seem cheery today."

"Oh yeah, it's always fun roasting people like that princess recruit." She shifted back into a soldier-like pose and coughed.

"Yeah…" Savanna turned back to Dri and smiled. "It's nice to put people back in their place.

Wow. For one of the smartest brains on the planet, Dri thought as they arrived, *you are oblivious.* She walked in front of Savanna to see if she needed to stall and sighed in relief. Everyone had shifted and was now cleaning up. Mace winked at her as Savanna walked past to her office. Dri saluted and jumped down to meet them. "So how's it going?"

Mace smiled and gestured behind himself, "Well, these guys are great, first of all. They followed instructions perfectly and they work so efficiently!"

"So before you go marry the entirety of F.R.E.E, care to

tell me what your progress is?" Dri shook her head.

Mace laughed and Zack took over explaining, "Well, we have enough for war. They're not polished, but they'll work. As far as transporting them secretly for each person...I'm not sure."

"Well, we could say that we need more help and then just tell everyone to take what they need to fight." Mace had stopped his nervous laughter to give a suggestion.

Dri pondered it for a little while, "I guess that could work...I will make an announcement."

After Dri had left Savanna passed by carrying some items in a box. Mace and Zach got everyone together and told them to take weapons for themselves while Dri sent people down. Within a few hours they had packed everything up and were heading out. Savanna walked around to make sure everything was loaded. While in there she ran into Dri, "What are you doing here? You're supposed to be monitoring out there!" She said.

"I am here to distract you." Dri replied, in a very monotone voice.

"You're not Dri..." She quickly raised her sword to block a hand swing. "Decoy robot..." Savanna swung her sword down to damage it. The robot took a hit to the knee and rolled out of the way of the next attack.

"You even fight like her!" Savanna commented as she jumped over its head and stabbed in the back. "Funny though, because you'll never be as fast as her."

The robot fell forward with a *clang* as Savanna ripped out its core. She then ran back outside to see most planes gone and

Dri about to leave with the last one. Savanna bolted through the closing door and grabbed Dri. Dri struggled away and jumped onto the helicopter. Savanna followed close by as they took off. "WHY DID YOU SEND A DECOY ROBOT AFTER ME?? WHAT ARE YOU HIDING?!"

Before Dri could answer, the pilot of the helicopter yelled back to them, "PENICH BUILDING IN TEN MINUTES!"

Dri sighed and closed her eyes as Savanna stepped back. The Penich building was mostly square, but short; most of its floors were underground in the dark. The outside looked like a pristine cube. To the normal eye, it would look like a glass block but to the trained eyes of the F.R.E.E. group, it was a reflective mirror blocking their goal. Penich's goal was to build a world where everyone followed orders blindly. Systematic and plain. They would choose simple minded people to say what they wanted. Most of these people were only there for the money and hated most of the population (Not to mention the discrimination against the neighboring planet, Mirenac, which consisted of blue skinned aliens). Savanna was leaning against a rail that was there for safety reasons, trying to assess the situation. "You...went directly behind my back...to go on a suicide mission...and wage an all out war against something we have no hopes of defeating?"

"Please, Sav, these are soldiers you've trained. They await your orders and if you don't like that then I will lead them because this is what it's been about. It's always been about this. You can argue it however you want, but I will still lead them like a true leader should." Dri stood firm where she was and gestured to the others around her while speaking.

Zach stood up and held a hand out to her, "Savanna, you know...Conner might be there...and I want to save him. I am willing to give my life for him. As long as I've known you, you have always encouraged change and breaking the social norm. Why now give up all we've worked towards because of the risk? You know this won't end peacefully."

Mace stood as well, "I haven't known you for long, but I can assure you that you will be a great leader if you tried."

Savanna sat down and covered her ears, "No no no...I can't lead, I'm not cut out for it. There is NO way that this could ever work with me leading you. Choose someone else; I am not going to lead you..."

Another F.R.E.E. member, Camille, walked over, "Come on, Boss, take your position. I know you want to." She smiled brightly.

Camille was known as the optimist and could get anyone to feel better. She was so charismatic that people just believed her positivity. Among others that soon arrived to urge on Savanna, the group was alive and buzzing with anticipation. Savanna tried to block them out, but it wasn't working, so she stood up and got a parachute. She looked at Dri and mouthed, 'I'm sorry' before jumping out of the helicopter and diving towards the ground.

The group looked towards Dri and she nodded, "We will still attack, with or without her. Get ready."

"TWO MINUTES UNTIL PENICH BUILDING!"

6.
ATTACKING THE ENEMY

The inside of the Penich building is not as pleasant as the outside. It lacked the sophisticated air that the outside held. The walls were covered with old wallpapers that were peeling away with the years. Mold covered the top of some of them. This only showed that they cared about their outside appearance, but of course they believed no one was going to see the inside, so why bother decorating? The rooms inside the building were pretty dull, only consisting of a desk and computer equipment. This was used mainly for reports. On the highest floor was the meeting room, this had all the main routers and connection servers. These servers were monitored by trusted employees and the whole thing run by Allen Jacobs. Allen Jacobs was a man that grew up in a system. Everything he did followed a schedule. He had typical male hair and wore a suit every day. Allen was obnoxiously cheery, though many people feared him; for he held the key to the torture chamber. That's what they called it, but it was less torture and more execution. Either you died or you betrayed your co-workers. Each exit did not allow you to be the same, so it was a death sentence anyway, internal or external. It held weapons of all kinds, but not the normal kinds. Most were barely recognizable as what they used to be. They had been altered to be deadlier and 'efficient' as Allen said.

Dri choose a group of people to be on lookout crew with her and they went first, giving instructions that if they did not return in an hour to leave the premises. The group consisted of Dri, Mace, Zach, Roxy, and Camille. "Alright, group, listen up." Dri stopped them outside the helicopters after they gathered weapons and put on armor, "The patrol takes them around the base and two squads around each floor, individually. If we time it right, we should be able to basically walk right in. I am unaware about any other protocols they might have, but Allen is a pretty old-fashioned guy, so I can't imagine much. Whatever it is, we must be prepared for it."

"What if they're all secretly zombies?" Mace asked clutching his gun closer to his chest and after receiving a few questioning looks he smiled nervously and said, "What? It was just a joke..."

"Don't joke in the middle of war!" Camille smacked his arm and pulled up her face mask, walking forward a few steps to peek around the corner.

"She's right." Dri shrugged.

Camille waved to the others to follow and disappeared around the corner. As they stepped behind her quietly, Zack looked at every directory and door to find the prison. Camille signed to Dri (As they both knew sign language), 'Prisons are normally on the lowest floors'

Dri slung her gun over her shoulder strap to reply, 'Yes, but these guys are unpredictable, now keep moving before we're dead, the next round arrives in a minute.'

Camille stood jogged to the stairway door and whispered to everyone behind her, "Roxy, come here. You have the lock pick in your hair."

Mace paused for a minute, "I thought we had some high tech gadget for that..."

"Yeah, but this is a regular lock." Zach walked closer to examine it, "This guy really is old fashioned..."

"Yeah...Roxy." Camille called out, to which there was no response, "Roxy? Roxy!"

They looked around, but Roxy was nowhere to be seen. Zach moved them out of the way and kicked the door down. "I don't care where she is, my boyfriend is in trouble."

"How cute!" Cheered a familiar voice behind them.

When the group turned around they saw Roxy with a bunch of guards, more of them running from various doors, "I love seeing the cute ones get protective. Also thank you for opening the door for us because prison is exactly where you're going!"

She smiled and clapped. Everyone was too stunned to resist the arrest. Except for Dri who was planning too many escapes and did not pick one out before she was handcuffed. She replied to this sudden restraint by mumbling, "Aw come on...!"

The first one to wake up was Zach, who had discovered the shackles around his ankles and set out to unchain himself, when it didn't work, he examined the others around him. Clearly someone had beaten them up. He guessed Roxy and continued looking. He noticed the cell next to him had a loose brick, so he pushed it out. Zach looked through and saw someone in ripped clothing. "Hey! Over here!" Zach whispered.

The guy looked over and his face lit up. "Zach! It's-It's me, Conner!"

Zach looked at him and held out his hand. "Oh my gosh...What did they do to you?" He said, referring to the cut across Conner's neck.

"That doesn't matter. We need to get you out of here before it's too long. They need you out there!" Conner started to bash at his shackles with the brick that fell.

"I just want you safe. The world can wait." Zach broke more bricks off and assisted him.

Dri woke up next and watched them for a while. She smiled at them being reunited then frowned at Roxy entering the room. Luckily, Zach and Connor put the bricks back when she entered. Roxy didn't notice. She walked straight to Dri's cell and peered inside. "I was hoping you were awake." Roxy laughed and when Dri didn't reply, she continued, "Anyway I need you alive...for now. So, do us a favor and give us what we want."

Dri refused to talk. Roxy glared and frowned. She slammed a crowbar against the cell bars and walked to the next one. Mace was facing the wall and wouldn't move, so she continued. She examined the containment, bored with all of them. Then she found Zach and Conner. Zach saw her look at Conner and grabbed her hair, smashing her head on the bars. The guards instantly pointed their guns at him as he spoke, "You leave him alone." He warned, "Or I will be your worst nightmare."

Roxy smiled and snapped her fingers. "Take Prisoner 6642."

Two guards walked in, armed with guns and aiming visors. One walked ahead of the other and took a chain of keys off of his belt. He unlocked Conner's cell and grabbed him roughly by the arm. Zach's protesting went unheard as they dragged him away. Dri watched in terror as the already hurt man was dragged as carelessly as a ragdoll. The other guard jabbed the butt of his gun at Zach to get him to release Roxy. When he did, Roxy scrambled back and hissed, "You better learn your lesson now because you will never see him again!"

7.
ESCAPE

Screaming. Screaming. Screaming. Screaming. Dri heard it all. The first to go was Conner. She didn't know what Roxy wanted with him, but he never returned. Then it was Zach who, since Conner's disappearance, had been trying every way of escape. He failed each time and was tagged as a nuisance and eliminated on the spot of his next attempt. Mace managed to get away when they came to get him, but there was no sign of him returning. Soon it was just Dri and Camille. Camille was standing and calculating the guards' movements, trying to escape. Dri was sitting on the ground, she had given up. Camille sighed, "Hey...we can't give up just yet, you know?"

"I failed. I tried to take Savanna's place and it didn't work. I should have listened to her." Dri leaned back on the wall.

"Yeah. You should have."

"Pardon?" Dri turned to face her cell.

"I'm not going to sugarcoat the truth. You probably should have listened. She's had more experience than any of us and it was a mistake to think we could just storm in here and win, but even then we didn't know Roxy was working with the bad guys." She shrugged.

"Huh…" Dri let out a broken laugh, "I don't think she knew she was working for them. Must have been some spell or just a really good ploy. She seemed normal enough…"

"That's not the point. You messed up, now accept it and

45

move on. We all do no matter how big or small, but you've got to move past it, Savanna's still out there!"

Dri smiled softly and thought for a moment, "You're a real good gal, you know that? You know your stuff for a rank three cadet. I want to move on...maybe I will, but Conner...and Zach. You're even here because of me, why don't you hate me?"

"I volunteered, it's my own fault that I'm here, but I wouldn't have volunteered if I wasn't positive that you could get me out." Camille laughed.

A few days later Camille was scheduled to be taken. The guards lead her away as Dri hid her face. Maybe five minutes later, alarms rang out; a sign that someone would soon be dead in Dri's mind. She heard shouting and gunshots in the hallway, *that's new*, she thought. "Stop moping around, General, and get out of the cage!"

Dri looked up and froze when she saw Savanna, her hair was gone and she had opened the door to Dri's cell. After realizing what was going on, she grabbed Savanna's hand and ran out with her. "Where are we going? What about Camille?"

"Don't worry about that. Knowing the location only puts you at risk for exposure if caught. Camille is on her way to her family." Savanna spoke quickly as they entered the forest.

Dri nodded and followed her without another word. They eventually made it to an old building, weathered by age. The roof was barely holding and only three walls remained. There were patches of grass and ferns sprouting through the cracks in the rubble. Savanna slowed to a stop and collapsed on the ground. She grunted and dropped her gun.

"Savanna! Are you ok?" Dri rushed to her side, alarmed.

"Yeah I'm fine." She smiled. "I need to lose weight though, I'm not in shape."

Dri laughed and lay down next to her. "What happened to you?"

"I could ask you the same thing." She motioned to Dri's tangled mop of hair, "I hid, had to change my look because people would know it was me. Or at least that's what I thought. Now that I think about it, I'm not too sure why. I think it looks nice, though. What about you?"

"As your second in command I'm obliged to say you always look nice. As your closest friend, I think you are lovely." Dri smiled at her.

"You're more than a friend." Savanna turned to lay on her side, so she could face Dri. "Anyway, I'm sure you have a million questions, so shoot."

"Ok." Dri turned as well, "What now? I mean F.R.E.E. is pretty much gone and Penich's pretty much won at this point."

"Let's take a walk." Savanna got up and waited for Dri.

Dri stood and followed Savanna as she led her to a cave. Dri watched the surrounding area before she actually noticed what was in the cave. Hundreds of crystals, Dri estimated, poking out of the walls of the cave. Savanna motioned for her to keep going and she took something out of her jacket. "This is a UV light bulb," Savanna explained, "It will shine throughout the area in all directions, unlike a regular UV light stick, so it makes this place beautiful. I mean, not that it's not beautiful now, but it just brightens it up."

"Beautiful?" Dri asked.

Savanna nodded and turned it on, suddenly, all the gems in the area began to shine back in marvelous purple and shades of dark pink. Dri gasped and smiled, looking around. "Fluorite!" Savanna whispered, "It glows under UV light."

Dri looked at Savanna and felt joy. Strange for everything that had recently happened, but she was ok. For just a moment, she was at peace. Being here, being with her, "It's absolutely amazing."

Savanna smiled and turned off the light, "I knew you'd like it. About everyone else, though, I have a plan, we'll gather them together, you and I, and we'll go in the same way I did. If we take out Allen, they'll be free, right?"

"Sounds awfully simple, but I guess we have nothing to lose." Dri nodded.

"I'll be right back; I'm going to get my gun." Savanna smiled and ran off to the building.

Dri waited for a while until she was positive that Savanna was taking too long. She walked back, ever cautious and stopped when she saw a vehicle parked outside the building. Dri walked to the back of the building and watched. Inside was Allen, holding Savanna's gun. In front of him were two guards, one holding onto Savanna. Dri glared at him and climbed in through the window and approached Allen. Luckily, the guards weren't paying attention until she kicked him in the back of the knee. "Whoa!" He exclaimed, "That's not very nice. Charlie, be a dear and get this one." He grunted from the ground.

Apparently, Charlie, the guard ran over and grabbed Dri

despite her efforts to stop him. He pinned her down as the other guard strengthened his grip on a struggling Savanna. Allen stood up and fixed his suit, "Now that that's settled, I will resume my general bad guy speech." He cleared his throat, "Blah blah blah, inhalation, blah blah blah, your doom, blah…blah…choose."

Dri looked at him, confused, he was serious about the choose part. "Choose what?"

"Oh! Whoops…see I like games, so I'm willing to play just one for now, but only one. I was going to just let her play, but now that you're here, we can play another game!"

"And what game would that be?" Savanna asked.

"Choose who will die now and who will have the chance to escape. Of course, since I plan to conquer this miserable planet, it probably won't matter if you get away and besides what's one person to a whole planet?" He laughed, throwing the gun up and proceeded to try and catch it. He failed, as it landed next to him, but he laughed only more because of it.

"I'll do it. I'll die." Dri said without hesitation.

Savanna looked over at her, "No!"

Allen smirked, "Eager. Alright, she's it."

"Wait! Isn't this a two person choice?" Savanna asked.

"Honey, I'm on a tight schedule. I've got shooting to do." Allen pointed the gun at Dri.

Accept it. The final step. I've messed up, I know, but there's nothing I can do about it. Except…there is. I can save her. That's all that matters. As long as she's safe…As long as she's safe…Bang.

ABOUT THE AUTHOR

A.M.Spadaro starting writing a young age. She would write whenever she desired and still continues to write to this day. Along with writing, she enjoys acting and drawing.

CPSIA information can be obtained
at www.ICGtesting.com
Printed in the USA
BVHW01s1124171217
503035BV00025B/2187/P